SAM PARROW AND THE TIME STONE TO BETHLEHEM

Sam's first exciting time travel adventure

Gill Parkes

ISBN: 9798736749539
Imprint: Independently published

Cover design by: Art Painter
Library of Congress Control Number: 2018675309
Printed in the United States of America

For my wonderful grandchildren - Annabelle, Grace, Sophie, Matilda, Madeleine and Noah

"We will not keep them from our children; we will tell the next generation about the Lord's power and his great deeds and the wonderful things he has done."

PSALM 78 VS 4 (THE GOOD NEWS BIBLE)

CONTENTS

MAP OF ISRAEL

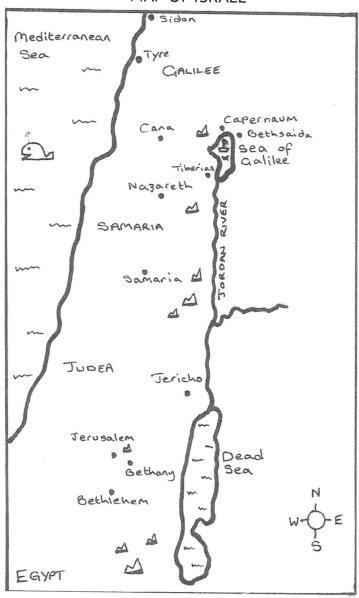

Sidon

Mediterranean Sea

Tyre

GALILEE

Cana

Capernaum

Bethsaida

Sea of Galilee

Tiberias

Nazareth

SAMARIA

Samaria

JORDAN RIVER

JUDEA

Jericho

Jerusalem

Bethany

Dead Sea

Bethlehem

N
W — E
S

EGYPT

LIST OF CHARACTERS

Ahab - *Servant*

Andy - *Sam's dad*

David - *Future King of Israel*

Eli & Jacob - *Rachel's brothers*

Goliath - *Philistine giant*

Jesus - *Messiah*

Joseph - *Jesus father*

Jo - *Sam's mum*

Mary - *Jesus' mother*

Matthew - *Rachel's son*

Ollie & Jack - *School idols and bullies*

Pharisees - *Religious group*

Rachel - *Shepherdess*

Sam - *12 year old time traveller*

Samuel - *Prophet*

Saul - *King of Israel*

Zaccheus - *Tax collector*

CHAPTER 1

Oh no, not again! Why couldn't they leave him alone? All Sam wanted was to get out of school, go home and read his new book. He'd got it from the library at the weekend but hadn't had chance to do anything more than flick through it – 'Time Travel, Fact or Fiction?' Okay, so he knew it was impossible but the illustrations were brilliant and well, he could dream couldn't he? What he wouldn't do to be able to go back to 1903 to see the Wright brothers first flight! How awesome would that be! Instead, he was stuck here listening to the taunts of Ollie and Jack, both good looking, athletic and adored by all the girls in their year.

Sam, on the other hand, was none of those things. With brown hair cut super short to prevent it sticking out every which way, muscles that even a mouse would be ashamed of and still the shortest boy in the year, Sam Parrow's nickname, 'Sparrow', was the obvious choice. His parents had thought it was cute, calling him Sparrow right from the day he was born. 12 years later however, Sam was inclined to disagree, especially when it was accompanied by insults from the school idols. Hoisting up his backpack, Sam ignored them and hurried home. The sooner he could lose himself in time travel the better.

Thankfully the end of the week came round quickly and with it, the half-term holiday. Sam grinned as he raced home to pack his rucksack, easily ignoring the usual jibes as he thought of the days ahead.

His parents owned a cottage by the sea in Norfolk and they'd been holidaying there for as long as he could remember. It was a ramshackle old thing, tucked in amongst the dunes at Sea Palling on the east coast. With two bedrooms, lounge, kitchen diner and shower room it was just about big enough for the three of them. There was a small porch where they could sit on a warm summer evening and a patio for the barbecue. But for Sam, the best thing about it was the dunes that backed right up to the fence with a long stretch of beach on the other side. The bays that served to defend Sea Palling from the destructive force of the sea were ideal for swimming, and although the North Sea was invariably cold except at the height of summer, it was great for surfing. Here his small stature didn't matter. He may not be the biggest or the strongest but his sense of balance was superb and the more time he spent on his board, the stronger he became.

After three days of catching the waves, Sam was beginning to get back into a good rhythm. Peeling off his wetsuit he shivered as the cool breeze met his bare skin. It was still not quite warm enough to be lying around reading a book! Pulling his hoodie on over his shorts, Sam decided to go for a walk.

Further north along the beach towards Happisburgh (weirdly pronounced Hays-bruh!) lay Eccles-on-Sea, most of which had actually fallen into the sea. The remaining village of small huts and cottages, some even smaller than theirs, was safely hidden behind a concrete defence barrier, erected in an attempt to keep the sea back from demolishing what was left. All along the east coast evidence of the sea's ferocity could be seen as more and more of the land was swallowed up. Rain, and the strong winds that Norfolk was known for, loosened the sand and soil of the dunes and small cliffs, sending landslips down to the beach, where the sea carried it away.

Sam often wondered where all the excess sand and soil ended up. He figured there must be a new country somewhere made up entirely of Norfolk land. Maybe he'd be the first to discover it like Christopher Columbus discovered America. He could name it Parfolk after himself and the place where the land originally came from. He would be king and the most important people would be the smallest. There would be laws to stop insults and all bullies would be banished. Sam nodded, it would be a good place to live.

Rounding the far corner of the last bay, Sam could see blocks and stones that were probably once a part of an old house that had fallen into the sea. Old Norfolk houses were made of brick and flint and many of the stones that littered the beach had once been a part of someone's home. Further along the coast broken pipes stuck out from the cliff and a shed hung precariously over the edge, its contents scattered along the shore. Here though, the sea had claimed most of what had fallen down and there was nothing left, apart from some oddly shaped stones.

Kicking over the largest one, Sam noticed another stone underneath. Something about it drew his attention, almost as if it was calling to him. Curious, he fell on his knees and started scraping away the sand around it until he was able to pull the stone out. Brushing off the residue of sand clinging to it, Sam turned his find over to inspect it thoroughly.

The size of a small juice carton, the stone was roughly rectangular, with one side a bit flatter than the other. On the flattest side were markings that looked as though they could be writing or some sort of decoration. It looked as though it may have broken off something and although Sam dug some more, nothing else came to light. Just then, a low growl came from Sam's stomach.

"I know, dinnertime," he answered the growl,

"I probably should be getting home." Putting the stone in his shorts pocket, Sam walked back to collect his board then climbed over the dunes to where he could smell the mouth-watering aroma of sausages cooking on the barbecue.

After dinner, Sam showed his find to his parents and they agreed that it looked as though it had broken off something, they just couldn't be sure what that something was. Firing up his computer, Sam typed Eccles-on- Sea into Google, adding lost artefacts to help with the search. He learnt that most of the original village had been lost, including St Mary's church which fell into the sea in 1895.

"Maybe it's something to do with the church," suggested his mum, peering at the strange carvings that decorated the front.

"Well if there was a church there would have been a graveyard," said his dad, "perhaps it's part of a cross or something." Changing the search to stone crosses, they straight away saw pictures of crosses large and small, old and new. Sam picked out some of the old ones and enlarged them for a closer look. One or two looked very similar to the stone that he had found although the patterns on them were very different.

"I wonder what the markings are," he said.

"Probably just decoration," said his dad, "any writing would have probably been on a plaque lower down." Satisfied that they'd solved the mystery, Sam shut down his computer and got ready for bed. All this fresh air along with his days on the beach was wearing him out. Besides, he still had his time travel book to read. Bidding his parents goodnight, Sam snuggled into bed with his book, the broken piece of stone on his bedside table.

CHAPTER 2

The hands on Sam's alarm clock moved round to midnight, and a strange humming sound nudged Sam awake. He had been dreaming about surfing the biggest wave ever and he could still feel the thrill of it. Opening his eyes he sat up and looked to where the noise was coming from. On his bedside table, the stone that Sam had found on the beach was emitting a faint hum. As he picked it up the stone began to glow faintly.

"What on earth?" he murmured, turning it over to see if there was a hidden switch that he'd missed earlier. The humming grew louder, filling his ears with sound, while the glow lit up the room with a strange blue light. Suddenly feeling dizzy and slightly sick, Sam shook his head and squeezed his eyes tight to try to regain his balance.

"Oh, wow!" he said when he opened them. Clutching the stone, which was now quiet and acting just like any other piece of rock, Sam gasped as he took in his surroundings. His bedroom had totally disappeared and in its place, he found himself sat on a grassy hill in broad daylight. Looking down, he saw that he was no longer wearing his pyjamas, instead he was dressed in some sort of knee length, brown wool tunic. There was a rope belt with a small leather pouch around his middle, and on his feet were leather sandals. Thankfully it was a bit warmer than a May day in Norfolk! Coming up the hill towards him was a girl dressed in similar fashion. She had long dark hair which was tied back in a braid and she carried a long stick with a curved top.

"Hello," she said, "have you seen a lamb wandering about? I've lost one."

"Er no," replied Sam, standing up so as not to appear rude, "I'll help you look though, if you like. I'm Sam." He tugged on his tunic, feeling a bit weird to be wearing a dress, but the girl didn't seem to notice anything wrong.

"Thanks," she said, a smile replacing the frown that she'd worn coming up the hill, "I'm Rachel." The children looked around at the sparse countryside but there was no sign of anything small, white and woolly. As they carried on looking, Sam tried to find out about where, and when, he was.

"So erm, where exactly are we?" he said.

Rachel looked at him curiously, "Just outside Bethlehem of course, where did you think we were?"

"Oh great, I wasn't sure, I'm new here," he stuttered, hoping she wouldn't ask too many questions that he had no idea how to answer.

"Have you come for the census?" she asked, "the town's full of new people. I've been sent out here with the sheep so that there's more room for my cousins. They've had to come from Jerusalem." Sam gasped; Bethlehem, census, seriously? Questions flooded into his mind like, how did he get there and how come they could understand each other? Then realisation dawned, the stone! It was a time machine!

Just then they heard a pitiful bleating coming from a thorn bush. Running over to investigate, they found a small lamb caught in the thorns. Every time he struggled to free himself the thorns gripped tighter on to his woolly coat.

"There you are!" cried Rachel, "you silly thing.

Why didn't you stay with your Ima?" Gently stroking the lamb to keep it calm, she asked Sam to pull the wool out of the thorns. It was not an easy task but her soothing voice kept the lamb still so that he could work. Eventually the lamb was free and Rachel picked it up, draping it over her shoulders so that it couldn't run off again. Seeming to know that he was in safe hands, the lamb settled down and went to sleep.

"Thank you, Yahweh, for delivering up this precious lamb to me. May your name be glorified forever," Rachel sang joyfully as they walked back down the hill. Not sure what to say that wouldn't cause awkward questions, Sam kept quiet. What was an Ima and who was Yahweh? Rachel seemed to think that Sam was there for the census so maybe he should just go along with that.

At the bottom of the slope a large flock of sheep grazed contentedly while their shepherds sat around a small cooking fire.

"I see you found him then," spoke one of the older shepherds who took the lamb from Rachel and inspected it for injuries.

"He was tangled up in a gorse bush," she said, "let me find his Ima, he must be hungry."

The older shepherd nodded, "He seems fine, a good drink of milk will satisfy him." Rachel took the lamb and went out into the flock, calling softly.

"There she is, standing alone crying for her little one." Placing the lamb on the ground, they watched as he ran over to his mother who baaed joyfully as the lamb suckled on warm sweet milk. "There, one happy Ima and her baby," Rachel turned back towards the shepherds' camp. "Thanks for your help. Stay and share our meal, my brothers won't mind, we have plenty."

Grateful for the offer, Sam nodded, "Thanks, I'd like that."

He realised that one of his questions at least had been answered, 'Ima' must mean mother or mum. He was glad he hadn't asked her that one, she would have thought he was crazy!

CHAPTER 3

The meal had been delicious, a thick vegetable stew, slightly sweet and not too hot. Sam thought he might ask his mum to look up the recipe when he got back. If he got back. He shivered as it suddenly occurred to him that he didn't know how to get home. What if he was stuck here forever? He felt for the stone that he'd kept safe in the small pouch tied to his belt. It was still acting very much like a stone and not a bit like a time machine. Maybe it had brought him here for a reason and whatever it was hadn't happened yet? Sam decided that there wasn't much he could do about it so he might as well act as though he belonged there. He was going to have to be extra careful and watch what everyone else did so as not to attract too many questions.

"Will your family be worried about you?" asked

Rachel, collecting up the cooking pot to wash in the stream. Sam got up to help, thinking hard about what to say.

"No, they'll think I'm asleep. As long as I'm back by morning it will be fine." Well at least he was honest, even if it wasn't the whole story! He looked around at the large expanse of grass surrounding them. "I like it here, it's peaceful."

Rachel laughed, "Yes the town is certainly very busy right now. I don't think they could even squeeze a mouse in!" Sam joined in her laughter and they quickly washed the bowls and cooking pot before returning to the camp. Stretching out on the grass they looked up at the stars, the only sounds coming from the sheep as they settled down for the night. One star seemed to shine a lot brighter than the others.

"That's new," said Rachel, "I'm sure I haven't seen that one before." A strange feeling came over Sam, he was beginning to think he might know when in time he had arrived. He thought about the stories that were told at Christmas. Could they really be true? In his last Nativity play in year 5, he'd been given the part of a shepherd. He'd felt a right idiot at the time, presenting a stuffed toy lamb to a doll in a basket. They'd not had to do it in year 6, they were supposed to be preparing for high school so they'd had a concert instead. If the stories were true they were probably due to see a host of heavenly angels soon, awesome!

A cool breeze blew over the camp and before long, the sounds of shepherds snoring joined the snuffles and bleats of the sheep. Sam closed his eyes and dreamed of lambs tangled up in Christmas trees.

Sam woke with a start. The area around the camp was lit up as though a thousand light bulbs had been switched on. The shepherds were all lying face down on the ground and beside him, Rachel was shaking with fear. The sheep however, were still fast asleep, unaware of anything strange that might be happening. Even though he thought he probably knew what was going on and what was about to happen, Sam felt just as afraid as Rachel. The light was coming from someone standing in front of them, someone who was huge and glowing like a beacon on overload. Sam marvelled at the angel standing before them. He was however, a little disappointed that he couldn't see any wings.

In a voice that was loud and clear and unlike any voice that Sam had ever heard before, the angel spoke,

"Do not be afraid. I bring you good news of great joy that will be for all the people. Today in the town of David a Saviour has been born to you; he is Christ the Lord. This will be a sign to you: You will find a baby wrapped in cloths and lying in a manger." Immediately, a whole army of angels joined the one who had spoken to them and they all began to praise God, saying,

"Glory to God in the highest, and on earth peace to men on whom his favour rests." When they had finished speaking, the angels left and the hillside was once more in darkness, lit only by the stars in the sky.

"Wow!" exclaimed Sam, visibly shaken by the experience. Rachel turned to him, a look of pure joy on her face.

"They spoke of the Messiah! We must go and see him!" Calling to her brothers, Rachel said, "Eli, Jacob, we must go to Bethlehem!" The shepherds agreed and together they set off down the hill towards the town.

"How will we know where to find him?" asked

Sam, "There must be dozens of mangers down there."

"Yes," agreed Rachel, "but only one will have a baby in it. Most of them will be filled with straw for the animals! I wonder if the new star will lead us?" Eli looked up at the star which shone brighter than all the others.

"It does seem to be moving," he said, "Perhaps we should follow it. The Lord sent his angels to tell us the good news. Maybe he sent the star to show us the way." Excited by all that had happened, Rachel, Sam and the shepherds hurried towards Bethlehem. It wasn't long before they saw the star appear to rest over a house near the edge of the town. Hurrying forward, they could see light coming through a small window so Eli knocked on the door. Speaking to the man who opened the door he said,

"The angel told us to come. He said we would find a baby, born tonight. He is the Messiah!" Opening the door wide the man invited them in.

"My name is Joseph," he said, "you are welcome here." Then, turning to the woman lying beside the manger he said, "Mary, we have guests, they speak of our son!" The shepherds followed the man into the lower room of the house which was normally reserved for the animals. Just as the angel had told them, a newborn baby lay in the animals feeding trough.

His mother smiled at them, "This is Jesus," she said. Rachel and Sam knelt down next to the manger, the shepherds kneeling behind. The shepherds told Mary all that the angel had said to them and they praised God for his goodness while the baby slept peacefully. When they left the house, they spoke to everyone they met, telling them what they had seen and heard and they all rejoiced that God had remembered his people and sent them their Saviour at last.

CHAPTER 4

As they walked back to the fields, Rachel and Sam talked about the angels and how everything they had said had been true.

"I've never seen an angel before," said Rachel, "they were amazing! I was so scared though."

"So was I," agreed Sam, "the one that spoke to us was huge!"

"And so bright! And wasn't the baby lovely, I wanted to cuddle him!" Rachel hugged herself as she imagined holding the baby they had just seen. Sam thought that was just typical of a girl, not that he would say anything. Mind you, even he admitted that it had felt special meeting the baby Jesus. He tried to remember the rest of the Christmas story, something about wise men bringing gifts. He wondered if they would get to see them too. The last scene of the school nativity had always seemed very crowded when everyone congregated on the stage. He didn't think the wise men would fit in the little house they had just left, especially if they came on camels!

Returning to the flock, Rachel made sure that the sheep were safe and that the lamb they had rescued was still with its mother. "There, none missing," she said, "Yahweh protected them while we were gone."

"Yahweh?" Sam was puzzled, who was this Yahweh Rachel kept speaking about?

"Yes of course, he sent his angels to tell us about the birth of the Messiah and where to find him. Because we listened and did as they said, he cared for our flock while we were away from them. He kept them safe for us."

Sam realised then that Yahweh must be the Hebrew name for God, but surely he wouldn't be bothered about a few sheep! Didn't he have bigger things to worry about? Rachel could see that Sam didn't really agree with what she had said.

"Don't you believe in him, Sam?" she asked. Sam hesitated, his parents didn't go to church and the only time anyone spoke about God was at Christmas and Easter. Or as a swear word - he certainly heard that a lot now he was in high school.

"Well, I don't really know much about him," he replied, "just a few stories like Noah and Moses." Sam was going to add, "and Jesus," but realised in time that those stories hadn't happened yet. His lack of knowledge could make things rather awkward for him. What on earth would Rachel say if she knew the truth? Even Sam had to keep pinching himself to be sure he wasn't dreaming.

Rachel obviously believed that God, or Yahweh, was real and after everything that had happened Sam was beginning to think she might be right. He just didn't know who God was. He thought he could accept that God had created everything, after all, they had to come from somewhere! The idea of everything starting up after a big explosion, somewhere in the universe, seemed impossible to Sam. There were too many things that needed to be just right for it to happen. Whereas a supernatural being that made them was a bit more believable - maybe. The trouble was, it was really hard to believe in something you couldn't see and who seemed too far away to take any notice of what was going on here. Besides, he prob-

23

ably had much more important things to worry about than the sort of stuff that bothered Sam.

Like the time when Ollie nicked his bike and then crashed it into his neighbour's rubbish bin. He'd run off laughing while Sam spent ages picking up all the rubbish. It was really smelly too, mostly old fish and chip wrappers, empty beer cans and used curry pots! Or when Jack had thrown his rucksack into a tree and Sam had ripped his trousers trying to get it back. He could have done with a God who was on his side then, he might not have got into so much trouble with his Mum for wrecking his trousers.

"Yahweh cares about all of us, even the smallest lamb in the flock," said Rachel, "We are all precious to him, that's why he has sent the Messiah." She thought a little more, in an effort to try to convince Sam that God cared. "It's like the lamb we rescued earlier. He was caught up in the thorns, just like we are caught up in our sins. We freed him and returned him to his Ima just like the Messiah will free us and return us to Yahweh's presence."

"But he's just a baby! What can he do?" exclaimed Sam.

"And you are just a boy!" declared Rachel, "But

one day you will do great things, Samuel, I'm sure of it." They both laughed, each of them thinking of all the things they could achieve when they were older, although Sam reckoned Rachel would be very surprised at the sort of things he was thinking about. Catching waves and flying planes was a very different world to the one he was in now.

Just then, a low hum came from Sam's pouch. Taking out the stone, Sam reckoned it must be time to go home. He wondered what Rachel would think when he disappeared! As he pulled it out, the stone began to glow with its strange blue light.

"Oh, what's that?" asked Rachel, grabbing his arm to get a closer look. Sam looked up in anguish. What on earth would she think if she ended up in his bedroom two thousand years in the future?

"No," he shouted, "let go!" He tried to pull away from her but it was too late. The sick and dizzy feeling he'd had the first time came back as the stone lit up their surroundings. The scenery changed and Rachel clung to him, open mouthed, as they looked around at the sight in front of them. The sheep had gone, but instead of being in Sam's bedroom, they were looking at a vast army standing at the bottom of the hill, facing an even bigger army on the other side of the field.

CHAPTER 5

Rachel was shaking, just as much as when the angel had spoken to them outside Bethlehem.

"Where are the sheep?" she whispered, "and who are they?" She looked as though she was about to cry and Sam realised it was time to tell her the truth. He really hoped she wouldn't freak out, he wasn't sure he could cope with a hysterical girl, he was having enough problems coping with it all himself.

"Er, I have no idea," he said, "But I think there's something I need to tell you." Sam carefully explained how he really lived in another country over two thousand years in the future and how the stone was a time machine that had brought him backwards in time, to the hill where he met Rachel. Rachel looked at him as if he'd grown another head.

"That's not possible," she said.

"Neither is being here, but here we are!" Sam

tried to laugh but he was beginning to feel a bit worried about having no control over the stone. Adventures in his own country in his own time zone were one thing, but this was an entirely different ball game. Rachel looked at the stone which was once more behaving like an ordinary rock.

"What are those markings?" she asked.

"I don't know, Dad thought they were just decoration."

"Does your family know you're here?"

"No. I really was asleep before I arrived on the hill. The stone woke me up when it started to hum. I was as surprised then as you are now."

Taking a deep breath, Rachel sighed, "I suppose we'll just have to make the best of it and see what happens. It certainly explains why you don't know much!"

Sam pulled a face, "I'd like to see how you'd cope if you ended up in my time!"

Rachel grinned, "Yeah sorry," she said, "It must have been really strange for you."

Sam returned the stone to the pouch and the two friends looked at the armies that were spread out in front of them. In the centre of the nearest one they saw a large tent where a tall man stood surrounded by guards. From where they stood they had a good view of everything that was going on, although they were too far away to hear what was being said. As they watched, they saw a boy approach the man and kneel in front of him. He didn't look as if he was a part of the army as he was dressed like they were, as though he too had just come from tending his sheep. After a short conversation the man spoke to one of the guards, who disappeared into the tent. When he came out he was carrying a spear and armour which he gave to the boy. He tried them on but the armour was way too big and the spear too heavy for him to carry. Taking them off, he stood up and spoke to the man again, then bowed before turning and walking towards the front line of the army. On the opposite side, at the front of the opposing army, stood a giant, over nine feet tall.

Rachel gasped, "It's David!" she said, "And that man by the tent must be King Saul!" Sam gulped as he realised that they had gone even further back in time. This must be where David had his fight with Goliath. Thank goodness he knew who won, otherwise he wouldn't have much hope for the boy working his way through the lines of soldiers.

As they watched, they saw David bend down towards the stream where he picked up some pebbles and placed them in his pouch, like the one that Sam wore on his belt. Sam smiled, at least he'd got that right when he'd put the time stone safe in his!

The giant moved closer to David, jeering and calling out insults for both armies to hear, reminding Sam of some of the insults he had to put up with. David replied with praise to God, declaring that it was the Lord who fought for Israel and who would give David victory that day. Calmly choosing a stone from his pouch he placed it in his sling as he ran closer to the giant. Swinging it around his head with practised ease, David let go and the stone flew towards Goliath, where it buried itself in his forehead. Rachel and Sam held their breath as the giant stood still, frozen to the spot. Then, after what seemed like an eternity, he fell face down with a loud crash. David ran over to him and heaving up Goliath's sword in both hands he killed him. David then used the sword to cut off the giant's huge head and held it up for all to see.

The children cheered as the Israelite army

chased after the Philistines, who turned and ran. In their excitement, it was some time before the children noticed that the stone was humming again. When they did, Rachel held on to Sam's arm as he took the stone out of his pouch.

"I wouldn't want to be left behind!" she said. Sam grinned and wondered where the stone would take them this time as the now familiar feeling of dizziness accompanied the next phase of their journey.

CHAPTER 6

They were standing on yet another grassy hill. Sam wondered if the stone had a liking for hills or if it was the same hill but at different times. This one did actually look very similar to the first one where he had met Rachel. Had the stone brought her home? Looking around he saw a flock of sheep but this time they were tended by a young boy. Rachel's brothers were nowhere to be seen.

"That looks like Bethlehem over there," said Rachel, "but it seems smaller. I wonder who that boy is? Let's go talk to him." As they approached, they saw that the boy was about their age and he was playing a small harp. "Do you have those instruments where you come from?" asked Rachel, "We call it a Kinnor."

"No," said Sam, "although I have seen pictures

similar to it on the internet. I think they're called lyres."

"Internet? What's that?"

"Ahh, that's really difficult to explain," answered Sam, "but it's how we find out a lot of our information."

"Do you not go to school? All the boys here attend the synagogue with the Rabbis."

"Yes, we have school and it's not just for boys, girls go to."

"Really? Girls attend school? Why? Our Ima's teach us all we need. We learn to cook, sew and to care for our families."

"Because where I come from, girls do other things besides looking after their children. My mum is a teacher." Rachel's eyebrows nearly got lost in her hair, she was so surprised.

"She must be highly esteemed," she said, "are you royalty?"

"Me?" laughed Sam, "You're joking! We're just ordinary, like everyone else. Most mums work, my aunt is a nurse and my gran works in a shop." Rachel thought about what Sam had just told her. It sounded as though life was very different in the future. She wasn't sure she would want to live in his time, she liked her life here.

As they got nearer to the boy, the sound from his harp flowed out around them.

"What a beautiful song," said Rachel, "may we sit and listen?"

"Thank you, sit here with me. I like to praise Yahweh while I tend my flock, it helps to keep them calm so they don't wander off." The boy sang as he played, bringing peace to the children after the excitement of the battle and the surprise of life lived in the future. Rachel sighed, it had been a very strange day and she wondered if there were any more surprises in store. She was certainly going to be in a lot of trouble with her brothers if she didn't get back to her own flock soon.

"David! David, come quickly. Your father requests your presence." A man ran towards them, calling to the boy who quickly stood and strapped his harp on his back.

"What's wrong Ahab, why the hurry?"

"Samuel is here, he wishes to speak with you. They are at the altar offering a sacrifice."

"Samuel, the prophet? He has come to my father? I must go. Stay with the sheep Ahab until I return." David hurried off in the direction of the town. Rachel jumped up, excited by this new development in their adventure.

"Come on Sam! Let's follow him, I know this story!" Sam got up and the two children followed David.

"Is this the same David who we've just seen kill a giant?" he asked.

"Yes, but he's younger! I think Samuel is going to anoint him as king!" Rachel laughed, eyes sparkling, "We've just been speaking to the greatest king who ever lived! That's why his song was so beautiful. He gave us most of our Psalms."

"Psalms?" asked Sam, "what are they?" Rachel looked at him sadly.

"Oh Sam, is Yahweh so forgotten in your time? The Psalms are the songs we sing in worship. They speak of the amazing things that Yahweh has done for us and they bring us comfort when we sorrow. Hurry, I don't want to miss this!"

They followed David to the sacrificial altar which was surrounded by a large crowd of men. They stood watching Samuel, who was speaking to David's father. Rachel explained that they were the elders or wise men of the town. Hiding themselves behind a bush, not unlike the one their lamb had been tangled in, Rachel and Sam were ignored by the men, who were far more interested in what Samuel the prophet was going to say.

"Abba, I'm here," David drew himself up in front of his father. Around him stood David's seven brothers, all older and most of them a lot taller. This time, Sam had no problems with asking the meaning of the word 'Abba'.

"It is an affectionate term for father," she said, "It is usually used by little children, but we all use it to show our love, even grown-ups." Sam was about to ask about the altar, which looked like a barbecue with a whole lamb cooking on it, when David's father began to speak.

"My son, Samuel has asked for you," then, turning to an elderly man standing next to him said, "This is my youngest son, David." Samuel stood quietly for a moment as if he was listening to someone no-one else could hear. Then he picked up what looked like a sheep's horn, tipped it up, and poured oil over David's head. The oil dripped down his face, running into his eyes and mouth. David bowed his head, as though he too was listening to some unseen being. The elders muttered to each other about the meaning of David's anointing. Rachel almost squealed with excitement.

"Shh!" whispered Sam, "They'll find us!" Hearing a noise, one of the men turned towards the bush where they were hiding.

"Oh no, he's coming over!" exclaimed Sam grabbing Rachel's hand and preparing to run. As he did so, the stone began to hum. Breathing a sigh of relief, Sam took it out of the pouch and as it began to glow, Rachel grasped his arm. Just in time, the stone whisked them away before they were discovered.

CHAPTER 7

"Baa," bleated the sheep as Rachel and Sam found themselves back amongst the flock they had left behind. The lamb was snuggled up to its mother and the bright star that had led them to the manger with the baby shone brightly in the night sky. Rachel's brothers were making their way back from the town, still rejoicing at all they had seen and heard.

"We're back at the same time we left!" exclaimed Rachel.

"Yes," breathed Sam with a sigh of relief. Maybe that meant he'd get home at the same time that he had left too. Suddenly, he felt a whole lot happier. Perhaps it would work out all right in the end. He looked at Rachel, "You're going to have to explain what was going on," he said, "None of it made any sense!"

"It must seem really strange to you. What would you like me to explain?"

"How about you start with that altar thingy? It looked like a huge barbecue cooking a meal big enough for a whole village!"

Rachel frowned. "I don't know what a barbecue is but the altar is where we offer our sacrifices to Yahweh. David's father offered a lamb as payment for his family's sins and to acknowledge that there is only one God, Yahweh himself. The priest kills the lamb then it is burnt on the altar. Yahweh accepts the offering and declares that those who offered it are free from their sin."

"So what did they do wrong? They didn't look like bad people."

Rachel shrugged. "Probably nothing more than any of us do. We are all sinners Sam. Every bad thought or wrong word is enough to keep us from the presence of God. The priests are kept busy making sacrifices for all God's people." Sam thought about all the insults and bullying he had suffered from Ollie and Jack. He reckoned they'd need a lamb each to pay for their wrong doings! His satisfaction faded though when he realised that his own responses hadn't always been as good as they probably should have been. If what

Rachel said was true, about even wrong thoughts keeping them from God, well, he was just as bad as they were. Not wanting to dwell on this anymore, Sam asked about the oil that the prophet had poured on David,

"And by the way, what's a prophet?" he asked.

Rachel laughed, "I hope the stone doesn't take you home for a while, you have a lot to learn!" Sam grinned, he certainly had, but he didn't mind staying. He liked Rachel, she was easy to talk to and didn't make fun of him for the way he looked. She accepted him for who he was, even though he must seem really weird to someone whose life was so different.

"A prophet is someone who hears Yahweh and then tells everyone else what he was saying. When Samuel was silent after being introduced to David, he was listening to the voice of God."

"How come we couldn't hear him?"

"Yahweh chooses who he speaks to. It is an honour to hear his voice but it is also a responsibility. He expects us to be obedient to him so it is important to listen well."

Sam nodded, he knew only too well how easy it was to make mistakes by not listening properly. Like the day he'd hurt himself the first time he'd got on his board. He'd been so excited to try it out that he hadn't listened to all the instructions. The huge bruise on his leg lasted the whole week of his holiday and stopped him from doing as much as he had hoped. He had made sure he listened to everything after that.

"Do you ever wonder what God said to him?" he asked.

"Oh, we know! It is written in the Torah." Seeing Sam's puzzled look, Rachel explained that the Torah was the collection of books that told the story of creation and the history of the Jewish people. It held their laws and the Psalms written by David. Sam realised that the Torah was probably the same as the bible from his time. Or some of it anyway, the parts that told about Jesus wouldn't have been written yet!

"So? What did he say?"

"Yahweh told Samuel to anoint David as king. That was why he poured the oil over his head, as a sign to say that he was the one that had been chosen to rule after King Saul."

"Didn't Saul have a son of his own? And surely it should have been the oldest who became king, not the youngest."

"In Yahweh's eyes, it's not age or size that matters, nor whose son or daughter we are. It's who we are ourselves that is important. Yahweh looks inside us and sees the good we have in our hearts and the way we would use that for the sake of others. He sees who we will become, not who we are now. David became the greatest king we have ever known. Yahweh saw his potential in the young boy who praised him as he cared for his flock." Rachel sat on the grass and hugged her knees. She smiled at Sam who had sat down beside her. "I don't know why you have come Sam, but I think Yahweh would like you to learn more about him while you're here."

Sam smiled, he was certainly willing to stay a bit longer now that he thought the stone would take him back to the same time he had left. He had already learnt a lot and he was looking forward to seeing where else the stone would take him. He was glad Rachel had been with him on the last two trips. Once she'd got over the shock she was just as excited as he was. It certainly helped to have her explain what was going on.

As her brothers got nearer, Rachel jumped up and ran to meet them. It was amazing! She'd just travelled a thousand years back through time and she wanted to tell them about meeting David and seeing him kill Goliath! Just then the stone began to hum and Sam realised it was probably time for him to go home too. He hoped Rachel would understand, especially as her brothers probably wouldn't believe her! Maybe the stone would bring him back again. Sam took it out of his pouch and waited for the dizzy, sick feeling as the stone began to glow.

CHAPTER 8

"Hey, watch out!" the boy next to him moved aside as Sam stumbled while trying to get his balance.

"Sorry," he said, looking around at his new destination. He wished Rachel was still with him but he'd been so sure he was going home that he hadn't waited for her to come back. He had no idea where he was, but it definitely wasn't his bedroom!

His clothes were the same so he must still be in Israel, he just needed to work out which time zone he was in. The stone had finally given up sending him to a hill, this time he was in the middle of a town and it was very crowded. All around him people were pushing and shoving and after the peace of the countryside, the noise was horrendous. Sam wondered if someone import-ant was about to arrive as everyone seemed to be looking in the direction of the gate at the entrance to the town.

"There he is!" someone shouted and Sam tried to see who it was but he was too short. Maybe he could climb the tree he was standing next to. He looked for a low branch to grab hold of only to see that someone else had had the same idea and beaten him to it. Oh well, he'd just have to stay where he was, there was no way he could push through all these people and he didn't want to cause any trouble.

At that moment the crowd in front of him parted, allowing a small group of men to approach the tree where Sam was standing. The one who seemed to be the leader of the group looked up at the man in the tree and smiled.

"Zaccheus, come down!" he said, "I must stay at your house today." The one called Zaccheus climbed down from the tree and stood in front of the group of men. Sam could see straight away why he had climbed up for a better view, he was almost as short as he was! Around him, Sam could hear people muttering.

"Why would he speak to him?"

"Doesn't he know what sort man Zaccheus is?"

"He's the worst sinner of all, why would Jesus want to go to his house?"

As soon as he heard the name, Jesus, Sam knew that he had jumped forward in time to when the tiny baby he'd just seen in the manger was grown up. To think that he had just come from seeing Jesus as a baby and now here he was, older, bigger and standing in front of him! This time travel stuff was awesome! He wished Rachel was here too but then, he realised, this hadn't happened yet for her. Maybe the stone could only take you back in time, not forwards. Sam guessed she'd be as old as his mum now. He wasn't sure he wanted to meet her as a grown up, she might not think that much of him! Sam wondered why the crowd didn't think that much of Zaccheus. What had he done that was so wrong, and why didn't Jesus seem bothered?

Zaccheus stood with his head held high and declared in front of the crowd,

"Lord! I will give half of my possessions to the poor and if I have cheated anyone out of anything I will pay them back four times the amount!"

Jesus laughed and said to him, "Today salvation

has come to this house, for the Son of Man came to seek and to save what was lost."

How Sam wished Rachel was here! He had no idea what was going on but he guessed that something important had just happened. He looked up to see the boy that he had bumped into when he arrived was watching him. Sam smiled, maybe he could explain?

"Hello, I'm Sam," he said, going over to where the boy was standing. He looked like he might be a little older being taller but Sam admitted that it was hard to tell, as most people his age were taller than him.

The boy grinned, "My name's Matthew," he said, "have you met Jesus before?"

"Er, no, he's not like other people is he?" Sam decided it was better not to mention he'd only just come from seeing him as a baby!

Matthew laughed, "No he's not. Ima is his friend, we're all part of the tribe of Judah. He's stayed at our house when he's visited Jerusalem for Passover. The things he says are amazing, he explains everything so you can really understand."

"What has Zaccheus done for people to hate him so much?" asked Sam.

"Oh, he's a tax collector, which basically means

he's stolen money off just about everyone here. Tax collectors always overcharge so only some of the money goes to the Romans, the rest they keep. Only Jesus could have got him to give it all back!"

"Do you think he will? Give it back I mean."

"Oh yes! Once you've told Jesus you'll do something you don't usually change your mind. He has a way with him that makes you want to keep your word. Look, why don't you come back with me and talk to Ima, she's really good at explaining things." Matthew grinned, he had an idea that his mother would be really pleased to see Sam.

Sam happily agreed, secretly hoping they would ask him to stay for dinner. A lot had happened since that delicious stew he'd eaten with Rachel and his stomach was beginning to growl again. After all, it was a very long time ago, he'd travelled back and forwards over a thousand years since then!

Matthew led the way through the streets to his home. The streets were narrow and the houses were similar to the house where Sam and Rachel had visited Jesus in Bethlehem. This town looked different though, older and maybe bigger, though it was hard to be sure. Sam wondered where he was but didn't think it would be a good idea to ask. He didn't think he was ready for the awkward questions and funny looks.

A delicious smell met them as they walked through the door. Sam's mouth began to water and he seriously hoped there would be enough for him to share.

"Ima, we have a guest," called Matthew leading Sam into the courtyard where his mother was stirring a cooking pot over a small fire. His mother stood up and turned to face the boys. She stood still for a moment taking in the sight before her. Then, wiping her hands on a towel tucked into her belt, she grasped Sam by the shoulders and smiled.

"Hello, Sam," she said, "it's good to see you again!"

Sam gasped, the woman standing in front of him was an older version of the girl he had first met on a grassy hill outside Bethlehem. "Rachel?" he said, "I've only just left you in the field with the sheep!"

She laughed, "That was over thirty years ago! I thought you'd gone home. My brothers didn't believe my story. They said I must have fallen asleep and been dreaming." She turned to her son, "How did you find him?"

"He bumped into me and looked as though he was going to be sick. I saw him put something into his pouch so I watched him to see what he would do next. It was obvious he didn't know where he was and he looked exactly as you had described him."

Sam blushed, "I still don't know where I am!" he said. Rachel laughed,

"You're in Jericho. I had hoped I would see you again sometime. I told Matthew all about our adventures when he became old enough to understand. I said that if he ever found anyone like you to bring them home."

"You're the fifth person I've invited. I'm glad I got it right this time!"

"You must be hungry, thirty years is a long time to wait for my lentil stew! Go wash your hands then come and eat."

CHAPTER 9

"Mmm, thank you, that was delicious!" Licking his lips, Sam pushed his bowl away and grinned at Rachel.

"You're welcome," she said, "I presume boys from the future eat just as much as boys do here!"

"Probably, but I expect your food is a lot healthier. I don't suppose you could tell me how to make it could you?"

Rachel laughed, "Are you going to surprise your Ima by cooking the meal for her?"

"Maybe not, but I could give her the recipe," Sam pulled a face, "I'm not really into cooking."

"Well that's no different to my son. Matthew would much rather be out in the fields than slaving away over a cooking pot!"

"Cooking is for girls," declared Matthew. "You are just complaining because my sisters are no longer around to help!"

"You have sisters?" Sam turned to Rachel in surprise, "How many children do you have?"

"Five - Simon is 26, Ruth 25, Sarah 22, Naomi 19 and Matthew here is 12, like you. I also have four grandchildren!"

Sam's eyes widened and his mouth dropped open in astonishment. He was amazed at the large family that Rachel had, especially as he had only just come from seeing her run to meet her brothers on that first Christmas morning. "Wow! Where are they all?" he asked.

"The girls are all married so they live with their husbands families. Simon is with his Abba, tending the flock, and his wife and children are at home with them in Bethlehem."

Sam looked puzzled, "So, you don't live here?"

"No, we are just visiting," replied Rachel, "my cousin has been ill and needed help with her children, they are all very young. Matthew came to keep me company on the journey."

Sam sat quietly, thinking about what Rachel had told him. The young girl he had left on the hillside just a short time before was not only married with children, she was a grandmother! This was seriously freaky! It was really good to see Rachel here but he had no idea why the stone had brought him to this particular time and place.

Matthew stood up, "Come on," he said, "you can sleep in my room tonight, there's a spare mattress." Rachel nodded and told the boys to go while she washed the dishes.

"And find a piece of pottery for me to write my recipe on. We can't let Sam go hungry!" The boys laughed and Sam wondered what his mum would think if he asked her to make lentil stew!

Jericho was situated on an oasis in the desert and felt hot and dry, so Sam was relieved to find that the bedroom was pleasantly cool. The stone walls of the house meant that the heat of the day stayed outside, making it more bearable to live there. Sam wasn't sure that he could live there permanently, being more used to the cooler climate of England. He was certainly glad to have been offered a cool room for the night.

Settling down to sleep the two boys chatted about their very different lives. Sam decided to avoid talking about things like cars and the internet. Some stuff was just too difficult to explain!

It did seem though that there were some things, people particularly, that didn't change. Some you liked, some you put up with and some were extremely annoying! Matthew was definitely one of those people he liked and as he drifted off to sleep, Sam hoped that the two of them were going to have some really good adventures! He felt sure that the times he had visited were all linked somehow and that the stone knew exactly what it was doing. Feeling confident that the stone would take him home when it was ready, Sam fell asleep.

On the floor between the boys' mattresses, the stone began to hum quietly. As it gradually grew louder the boys woke up and Matthew looked at Sam, wide eyed with excitement. "I was so hoping I'd get to go on a trip with you," he said. Sam grinned as he picked up the stone and just like before, a strange blue light filled the room.

"Hold on, don't let go," he said to Matthew and his stomach did a somersault as the room disappeared.

"Woa!" cried Matthew as he fell against Sam, "no wonder you bumped into me when you arrived!"

Sam laughed, "I think I'm beginning to get used to it now. That wasn't anywhere near as bad as the first time." He looked around at the place the stone had brought them to. "Do you know where we are?" Matthew looked up and considered their surroundings. It looked similar to Jericho but smelt different, sort of fishy. It felt slightly cooler too.

"No, I don't recognise it but look, there's a crowd of people over there. Let's go and see what's going on."

The two boys walked over to the town square where a number of people were gathered. Pushing their way through to the centre, they saw Jesus surrounded by his friends and various groups from the town. One group looked very officious, they seemed to be looking down their noses at the other people who were listening to what Jesus was saying.

"They're just like the men who were saying stuff about Zaccheus," said Sam as he heard them put down the rest of the crowd who were listening.

"That's because they're all Pharisees. They think they're better than everyone else."

"Who are Pharisees?"

"Religious fanatics. They make rules about keeping rules so it doesn't matter what you do, you know you're going to break them. It's impossible to keep every rule they say we should."

"So why do they make them then?"

"Probably to make themselves look good. They spend their whole lives showing people just how law abiding they are."

Sam thought they sounded very like the school bullies back home. He wondered what Jesus made of them all. He was soon to find out, Jesus had heard what was being said and as he so often did, he spoke to the crowd with a parable, a special story that had a meaning for that situation.

"There was once a sheep that had strayed from the flock," began Jesus. The crowd quietened, eager to hear every word the Rabbi spoke. "When the shepherd realised there was one missing, he left the ninety-nine sheep in the field and went in search of the one. When he found it, he carried it on his shoulders and returned to the flock. The shepherd was very happy and called all his friends and neighbours together to celebrate the return of the sheep that was lost. Listen to what I say, there will be more happiness in heaven for one sinner who repents than for all those who do not need to."

"Wow, that was just like the first time I met Rachel!" cried Sam, "She was looking for a lamb. We found it in a thorn bush and she sang all the way back." Matthew nodded.

"That's because even the smallest one is valuable," he said, "and to lose one is costly. That's why shepherds are so protective of the flock. It's an important job. I'll have my own flock one day, just like Abba and Simon." Matthew was obviously very proud of his father and brother and was looking forward to going back home to join them. Right on cue, the stone began to hum.

"Time to go," said Sam, and closing his eyes to avoid the dizziness, held on tightly to his new friend.

CHAPTER 10

The stone had brought them back to the bedroom they had just left. It was still dark, so the boys settled themselves down, and although they were both full of excitement at seeing Jesus, they very quickly went back to sleep. The next morning they jumped out of bed and ran to find Rachel to tell her of their adventure.

"I thought I heard a noise," she said, when Matthew excitedly told her about his first experience of time travelling. "I did wonder if the stone would whisk you away somewhere!"

"I don't think we went very far back though. Jesus looked just the same as he did yesterday when he spoke to Zaccheus, but I've no idea where we were. I didn't recognise anything."

"His home is in Capernaum so he travels around Galilee a lot. You were probably in his home town or one of the nearby villages."

"I think it was too big for a village. It looked very busy and it definitely smelt of fish!" Matthew wrinkled his nose, he much preferred the smell of sheep!

Rachel laughed, "Well some of his disciples are fishermen. Jesus stays with them when he's not travelling. It sounds as though that's where you were."

"Capernaum's miles away, it would have taken him days to walk here, especially if he stopped at other places on the way."

"Maybe he should get a time stone!" Sam said grinning, "It's even faster than the jets that fly over Norfolk!" Too late, Sam realised that he had spoken of things that were totally beyond his friends' understanding. Matthew punched him in the arm playfully.

"Maybe I should come with you to your home one day," he said. Sam smiled, he really didn't think that would be a good idea. There was some stuff you needed to be prepared for!

"Sit down boys, you can tell me what Jesus said while you eat breakfast."

As the two boys ate yoghurt with dried dates and figs, they told Rachel what they had heard.

Sam was amazed at how Jesus' story was so like

their first meeting on the hillside.

"But what did he mean when he spoke about happiness in heaven when a sinner repents?" he asked. Rachel thought carefully, she knew that the things Jesus said were important and she wanted to be sure she explained properly.

"I think it's all about how precious we are to Yahweh," she said. "He loves us so much that every time someone says sorry for doing wrong, and means it enough to try to stop doing it, the angels rejoice because that person has come back into Yahweh's presence."

"You told me the first time that even our bad thoughts are enough to keep us away from God. Are you saying that just being sorry is enough to get us back?"

"It is if you mean it. You can't just say it with your mouth but think something different. You once asked me why David had been chosen as king and I told you it was because Yahweh saw his heart. He saw that it was good and that David would stay faithful to God."

Matthew nodded, "I remember when Jesus came to stay when I was little. He was travelling with his brothers to Jerusalem for one of the festivals. I think he lived in Nazareth then, that's almost as far away as Capernaum. It's where he worked as a carpenter. I was upset because I'd found a baby bird that had fallen out of its nest."

Rachel smiled, "Yes, you cried because the bird couldn't fly, it had hurt its wing. I remember you were very cross with Yahweh for letting it get hurt!" Matthew's face went red.

"I was only four! Anyway, Jesus was really kind, he explained that Yahweh loved even the tiniest sparrow and he cared about everything that happened to them."

Sam sat up straight, he suddenly felt a bit weird, as though this story was especially for him. Matthew carried on, not noticing that his friend seemed to be paying more attention.

"I said I was sorry for being cross and Jesus said that Yahweh understood and that he was sad that the bird was hurt! I thought at first that Jesus was just saying that to make me feel better but then he gently took the bird from me and held it in his hands. He held it up to his face and the bird looked at him as though it was listening." Matthew shrugged, "You know, how they put their heads on one side sometimes? Then it flew away."

"You mean it wasn't really hurt?" asked Sam.

"Oh, it was definitely hurt. I think Jesus asked

Yahweh to heal it and he did."

Sam thought about the things that Matthew and Rachel had said. He supposed that God would care about everything he had made, even the small stuff. He also supposed that God wouldn't like it when they did things he'd told them not to. Maybe if God was real, he cared about Sam too. He certainly had a lot to think about.

Matthew went out to the courtyard to help Rachel put wood on the fire. Alone in the house, Sam picked up a pottery shard that was on the table. He grinned to see that Rachel had written the ingredients on it for her recipe. As he was going out to ask what they used to write with the stone began its low hum. Sam took it out of his pouch and its blue light lit up the room. Within seconds Sam was back in his own bed, the hands on his clock just past midnight. Although sorry not to have said goodbye to Rachel and Matthew, Sam was very relieved that the stone had brought him home. He hadn't wanted to spend the rest of his life jumping from one time zone to another! Placing the now silent stone on his bedside table, Sam settled down and went to sleep.

CHAPTER 11

Over breakfast, Sam tried to find out what his parents thought about God. It had never been a subject they'd discussed before, except to argue over whether or not they should go to church at Christmas and Easter.

"What's brought this up?" asked his dad, buttering his second piece of toast. "Pass the marmalade please, Sam." Sam replaced the lid on the jar and passed the marmalade across the table.

"It's that stone I found on the beach. It just got me thinking." Sam wasn't ready yet to tell them about everything that had happened the night before. It was unlikely that his parents would believe him, they'd probably say it was just a very vivid dream. He wasn't entirely sure he believed it himself!

"Well, a lot of people do believe in God," said his mum, "I don't suppose I've ever really thought about it. Too many other things to think about like work and your grandparents and what to cook for dinner."

Andy, Sam's dad, got up to get the teapot from beside the kettle. "I suppose it's something we ought to think about at some point. It would be nice to know there's a place in heaven for us one day. More tea Jo?"

His mum raised her eyebrows along with her teacup. "Plenty of time for those sort of thoughts, don't you think? I plan on staying around for a good while yet!"

"Good, because I plan on having a nice long retirement with plenty of time to watch the cricket."

Sam rolled his eyes. Trying to get his parents to be serious while on holiday was impossible. He supposed this was the only time they were able to relax away from the hustle and bustle of work and they intended to make the most of it. He didn't blame them, he hardly ever saw them at home. They were either working or looking after his elderly grandparents. Sam excused himself and got ready for another day on the beach.

The day was bright, sunny and calm. Sam hopefully carried his board over the dunes but the gentle lapping of the sea meant that surfing was an activity for another day. Instead, he swam a few laps around the bay, then lay on top of the board and watched the clouds slowly drift across the sky. In the broad light of day, the events of the night before seemed even more like a dream and Sam was beginning to think that's all they were. He had woken to find his time travel book open at the chapter about going back in the past to significant events. He must have fallen asleep while reading it and his imagination had done the rest. The stone was still on his bedside table looking like nothing more than a broken piece off a small cross. Sam figured that was probably why he'd been thinking about bible stories.

So why could he remember the conversations as if they had really happened? Everything had seemed so real, even Rachel's stew! Turning himself over, he paddled lazily around the bay, looking for fish. He wondered what his mum would make of it if he told her. She'd probably say he'd been dreaming and being a teacher, she'd tell him to write it down in an essay! Weird how it was making him think about God though.

Did God really care about him? Was Sam Parrow as precious to God as the lost sheep in the story? He thought about boys like Ollie and Jack who seemed intent on making his life miserable. Did God care about them too? Sam supposed he must - if he cared about the tax collectors and sinners he'd care about the name callers and bullies. So where did that leave him? It was all very well God caring about everybody but it didn't help when Sam got into trouble for ripping his clothes.

Maybe he should start going to church. Alex had asked him a couple of times to go to the local youth group with him. Sam had always said no, privately thinking that Alex was a bit of a wimp. But if our thoughts are just as bad as the things we say, didn't that make Sam as bad as Ollie and Jack? Perhaps when he got back to school he'd speak to Alex and ask if he could go along. There must be someone there that could answer his questions. Sam really wished it hadn't been a dream. He would have enjoyed getting to know Rachel and Matthew. Being able to really travel through time would have been awesome!

Eventually, the inevitable growl of Sam's stomach told him it was time to go home. Making his way over the dunes he made plans for the rest of the holiday. They hadn't been to check on the seals yet, he wanted to see how many babies had been added to the colony at Waxham. It was brilliant how they all congregated on the beach. You couldn't get too close though, especially when there were young ones around. The mothers were very protective of their young and would attack if they thought their babies were in danger.

The smell of cooking reached Sam's nose, causing him to stop in his tracks. "That smells familiar," he thought, "no, it can't be. It must be coming from somewhere else." Sam headed for the shower to make himself respectable for dinner.

"Mmm, smells good," said Andy appreciatively, "what is it?"

Sam pulled his chair up to the table and sat down. "It looks like lentil stew," he said, "You've never made that before, Mum."

"How did you know?" asked Jo, "Whenever did you eat lentil stew?"

"Err, I suppose we must have had it at school,"

replied Sam puzzled. It really had been a dream hadn't it?

"I found a piece of pottery on the floor by your bed, Sam." Jo continued, "There was a list of ingredients written on it. I assumed it was a recipe so I thought I'd give it a go. Try it, tell me what you think."

Sam almost choked on a piece of carrot. The pottery shard, he must have brought it back with him! He really had been to Bethlehem!

"It's delicious Mum," he grinned, "what did you do with the pottery?"

"Oh, I left it by your stone after I copied the recipe into my book. It's amazing, the pottery looks really old but the writing looks as if it was done yesterday. I'd love to know what they used for ink."

Sam felt a shiver of excitement, if only she knew! Scraping up the last spoonful of stew, Sam thought about the adventures he was going to have. He would go to the youth group with Alex. He would find out as much as he could so that the next time he saw Rachel he could show her how much he had learnt.

With dinner finished and everyone agreeing it

was one of the best meals they'd had, Sam went off to his room. Picking up the shard of pottery, he thought about Rachel, Matthew and the adventures they'd had. Then he realised, if they were real, then God must be real too! Not only had Sam been present at the very first real live nativity, he'd heard Jesus speak when he was grown up. And Sam had even spoken to the future King David!

If the things Rachel had said were true, then Sam felt certain that God knew all about him. And just as Jesus had cared for the baby bird when Matthew was young, he knew that God cared even more for a boy called Sparrow.

RACHEL'S LENTIL STEW

Serves 4

Ingredients

1 onion, chopped

2 sticks celery, chopped

2 carrots, sliced thinly

1 ½ cups red lentils

1 clove garlic, chopped and crushed

1 tbsp olive oil

1 tsp cumin

½ tsp coriander

2 tsp parsley

600ml vegetable stock

Salt and pepper

Method

Gently fry the onions and garlic in olive oil until soft. Add cumin and coriander, cook 1 min. Add celery, cook gently for 2 minutes. Add the rest of the ingredients, bring to the boil and then simmer for 30 mins until lentils are soft. Stir occasionally and add more water if necessary. Season to taste.

Serve with crusty bread.

GLOSSARY

Abba - *Dad, daddy*

Altar - *Large table where offerings are made to God*

Census - *Official count of the population*

Disciple - *Student of a Rabbi*

Ima (Ee-ma) - *Mum, mummy*

Israelites - *God's chosen people*

Kinnor/Lyre - *Harp, a musical instrument*

Messiah - *Saviour of the world*

Passover - *Jewish celebration held in Jerusalem*

Philistines - *Israel's enemy*

Prophet - *Someone who hears God and speaks
on his behalf*

Psalms - *Book of songs and poetry in the Torah*

Rabbi - *Teacher*

Repent - *Being really sorry*

Sacrifice - *Giving something up that is valued*

Synagogue - *Place of worship*

Torah - *Jewish bible*

Tribe - *Clan/extended family*

Yahweh - *God*

BIBLE REFERENCES

If you would like to read about the events that Sam visited you will find them in the Christian bible. There are lots of different translations but one of the easiest to understand is the Good News Bible.

Old Testament stories
David and Goliath - *1 Samuel ch 17 vs 32 – 51*
David's anointing - *1 Samuel ch 16 vs 4 – 13*

New Testament stories
Christmas story - *Luke ch 2 vs 8 – 20*
Zaccheus - *Luke ch 19 vs 1 - 9*
The lost sheep - *Luke ch 15 vs 1 – 7*

THANK YOU!

This is my first ever book and I want to thank all those who prayed for me and encouraged me along the way. I especially would like to thank Wendy Blackman and Catherine Metcalf and my wonderful husband Martin, whose technical skills helped to make it happen!

Of course, I must also thank Jesus, who inspired me to write and without whom I couldn't do anything.

Thank you too for reading, I hope to meet you again in the next one!

ABOUT THE AUTHOR

Gill Parkes

Gill Lives in Norfolk with her husband and enjoys walks along the beach and exploring the country-side. She loves to spend time with her grandchildren, especially snuggling up with them to share a good book.

Jesus is her best friend and she hopes that by reading these stories you will get to know him too.

Printed in Great Britain
by Amazon